AF596191

Preface

The poems you now are about to read are all the poems I have written, including the ones published as Poetry I-VI at Amazon.

Most of us write prose easily and quickly. Poetry writing is different. You have to rewrite them a number of times. Especially if you are about to write poems with rhymes and with short lines and simple words. Encouraged and impressed by the masters of the metric rhymes. You may wonder if the bunglers of free verse are going to bring poetry to the edge of the precipice.

In case you want to learn more about poetry I can recommend Gotham Writing School in New York, where you can take poetry courses over the Internet. I've attended Poetry I, Poetry II and a special course referred to as Poetry III. Just prepare yourself that it will take you almost full time during one solid month.

If you would like to comment or criticize my poems, you are most welcome. I'm fully aware of the fact that I have a slightly dirty mind.

Gunnar Barkenhammar

August 2020

gunnaratbarkenhammardotnu

A Man in your Drawer

A Man in your drawer
To pick up when you want him
To enjoy him when he's nice
To put him back when annoying

A Man can be wonderful
Good to have by your side
A Man can be terrible and
Deserve the time in darkness

A Man can be handy
For fixing a fuse and
For doing the dishes
When done he knows his place

A Man in your drawer
For the good moments
And back again
When things turn not so good

A Man can be good at parties
Dinners and discos
But when misbehaving
Sentence him to the drawer

A Silly Poem

When I get into thee
What kind of stiffness do you prefer
A hard 4U or a not so hard 4B

All the senses have voted for you

The vision because you are a Beauty
The hearing because you have such a
Sexy Voice
The skin because of your Vibrations
The balance because you are such a
Realistic Woman
The brain because you are so Brainy
The sex because you are so Good in
Bed
The taste because your Smell of Honey

Altruistic egoism

You tell me you love me
Highly appreciated words
I tell you that I love you
You look pleased
Do I love you if you don’t love me
Could it be that I love me
And you just confirm that love

Always on the run

Always on the run
Looking for something better
Never totally satisfied
Always in search for excellence
Anxious to get things done
Worrying for days to come

Always there

Always there
Right by your side
Always supportive
Always warm and smiling
Always a hand to hold
Come rain, come sunshine

Ambiguity

It wasn't too good
It wasn't too bad
We never got close
It just hurts to loose

Practical rationality or
Impractical irrationality
Settled by
Emotional chemistry

Our perfect match
Turned to a mismatch
Free wants tied and
Tied wants free

Without hell, no heaven
Dear moments
Paid by rough when
Going gets tough

The security addict
Seeks security in
Bad relation for sure
Predictable

Scanning for that
Perfect match
Out there to catch
Someday but not today

And why

Jobless and homeless
Mistrust and distrust
Apathy in futility

The Social control
Eliminated

Why bother

No dream
No aim
No future

Another kick
Towards polarization
Them and we

Apple-Worms

Only ghosts are left
In Kamikaze pilot's
Brainwashed brains
Whose ticket reservations to Paradise
are
Supported by
The left-wing intellectuals

Nothing new under the sun of sects
Same fundamentalist hedge horizon
Same Lenin transformed to bin Laden

The hard-core inner cirque
Trading casualties
For pure profit
Under a Mecca and Medina cover

The Star War
Cut down

To skyscraper level
Obsolete
Like the Polish cavalry
Against the machine gun

Authorities' Duties

Authorities' duties
To nurse and disperse
To give and forgive
To prize and surprise
The inherited set

Ballet and ballgames

Ballet and ballgames
Fine art and handicraft
Critics and comments
Fashion and folklore
Snob-culture and slob-culture

Bottomspotting

The fruit bound
Bottom beauty
Like apple and pears,
Pair of pumpkins,
Melonmolded, lemonlike
Squash shaped juicyloosy
Unripefirm pielikeflat
Cherrysized or eggplantlong
Cellulitis prune stuffed
Corset canned
A ruck pluck plum
Splendidly fullended
Asstronomic and rubenesque
Loose swinging ruralesque
Hedge hatch cut
Dew drenched fresh
Falling ripe

Breaking up

There is a price tag
On tearing down
There is a price for building
Flower beds have to be weed out
To let the flowers grow
Behind Scylla and Charybdis
Something new will show up
The tearing hell
To break the habitual
To get rid of
An obtuse discontent

The Breakthroughs

Five thousand years
It took to
Match the wheel
Now
We couldn’t care less
About the wheel
With the world at
Dashboard distance

The Butterfly flicks along the Main Street
on a Sunday Service Morning

The butterfly flickles
On his own funny way
Hap-hazardly
Through the straight city streets
Guarded
By solid brick walls
Designed
By law and order architects
Attending
The Sunday Service
The true sane
Flutters freely

Calls to Make

Calls to make
Calls to take
Phones demanding
Boss commanding
Meetings to attend
Contracts to amend
Coffee breaks to break
Turning points at stake
More disappointments
Than appointments
Puppet on a string
Let them bells ring
Visions will die
Moments go by

The Candle Crowned Queen

Ominous orbit overlooking-
Dusk dwelling deep down
Mastering moody mankind
Spirit from spirit splitting

Fellow fighting fellow
Family fighting family
Duels ending dear ones
Prince of Darkness praising

Candle Crowned Queen's
Serene steps
Foot by foot affrights
Darkness' domains

Flames fire flames
Kindness kindles kindness
Spirits inspire spirits
People are people's pleasure

Candy

Eyes sparkle
Breasts nipples
Hips sway
Inviting encouraging

Hands meet lips meet
Fingers find neck hair
Body close to body
Genitals feel genitals

Caress over
Soft buttocks and
Hairy pussy
Buttons unbuttoned

Erected and excited
The coq seeks an opening through
Wet pubic hair between
Widespread legs

Increasing speed
Gentle euphony towards
Ejaculation and orgasm in
Synchronized climax

Drained dick
Diminutive and drowned in
Fishy juice
Locking legs beg for more

Christmas Time

Now the Christmas time is here
Now the women peace is near
Each and every candle stick
In the window does the trick
Each and every little ball
For the Christmas tree enrol

Compact Living

The computer screen
Is the peephole
To the world's
Facts and fiction
Face book friends
Opinionated bloggers
YouTube movies

Keyboard clicks
Play on playgrounds
Date the dates
Chat with chatters

A compact living
Solitude social turns
Cyberspace somebody

The Cookie Container
Keep it out of reach in the Cupboard

Behind Scylla and Charybdis is
A new wonderful tomorrow
Refrain like Odysseus from
The immediate pleasure
By tying the coq to the mast

Cocooning Security

Baby blanket, beddiebyes
One more time the beddy
rhyme
Tied to those our lost and
gone
Child of warm and inner
cirque
Hand in hand the small in
big
Schooldays homework hide
and seek
End of week allowance paid
Food and garb a tent for
twelve
World so small with borders
sharp

Test, protest and parting
fear

Cracking shells from inside
out
Like the hatching chickens
do
Hedge horizon, rural views
Unsafe unsure, coq-sure
Deadline stress routines
demands
Grown-ups giving in and up
Masques and walls to hide
behind
Lost illusions gone too soon
Week and wage to match by
end

Security addicts
Seek refuge
In mentors and work
In parish and play
In networks and
brotherhoods

Cocooning Security
Written in a different way

The confined comfort passed and gone
Replaced by restless rest
In short-term shelters
The recognized identity
Engaged in chameleonic roles
On sundry stages
Relaxed ignorance
Replaced by global concern
For unknown fellowmen
The homespun ordinary
Distressed by cultural complexity
Compassionate conservatism
Is facing hard core capitalism
Mates for the occasion
Instead of good, old friends
Scattered dwellings referred to
As a place called home
By a past boundary marker

32

The cocooning security
Has turned to fictional freedom
Cultural change and
Prospective progress

The Countryside

Small villages
Small minds
Cow company
Scarcely creative

Local paper
Local news
Hedge horizons
World epicenter

Flower power
Redneck culture
Cleritocrazy
Ministeration

Gas station
Far away
Tank empty
By return

EU grants
Social allowances
Unproductive
Farmer's income

Rural cocksure
City stressed
Seeking security
Farm refuge

Latest fashion
Reach village
Out of fashion
City claims

Tractor pulling
Favorite sport
Big shot
When winning

Disco dancing
Harmonica music
Cross road floor
Miles away

The Crook Community. Haikku

Crook Community
Is where the subjects sleep
With their bicycles

Culture

The culture carrying women
In their upper mid-age
Candidly ingest
The quasi intellectual critic's
Premature comments about
The subsidized snob-culture's
Latest swan dance
With a certain feeling of being
Superior to their slob-cultural sisters

The Cultural Inheritance

Release our creativity from
The prejudging fundamentalists
Unshackle us
From the clerical burdens
Hampering our free thinking

Cycles

Fashion has been fashion before
Flames will be flames ones more
Good times follow rough and dusk
dawn
Previous experience shown
Sunshine follows rain and light nights
Making those sinus curved rites
Same amount of sweetness and lime
Cycle length a matter of time

Nothing is new under the sky
Diehards like we repeatedly try
Only the perspectives are new
Pathway and direction, we go
New is in the view of the minds
Place and time bringing different kinds
Track bound in a helix we strive
Upwards we renewed will revive

Every innovation to be
That's a combination, you see
Whose parts are already well know
Recombined to mixture unshown
Adding for the better or worse
Knowledge to our universe,
Simplifying complex-built ins
Trimming the surplus and the sins

The Divine Pope

Who art in the Vatican
Even so in Argentina
Save the choir boys
From pedophile priests
Let your sisters decide
When to have babies
It brings more bliss to give than to take
But not for your hypocrite brothers
Forgive your trespasses
As you are only a puppet on a string
For the Conclave

Donotfat

Battleshiplike
She's rollingly
Cruising
Sweatdrophot
Fatpadsplashing
Trapeziumdressed

Channelzapping
Consuming
Chips and Cola
Cocooning
Escapistic
Disillusioned

Her corporeality
Has turned her
Prison
Millstoneheavy
Maintenancedemanding

Locomotiondisabling

Lovesick
She’s missing hugs
And tenderness
Classindicated
Stigmatized
Persona non grata

Don't Wake Me Up

Don't wake me up
I'm bound for heaven
Don't make me face
The morning light

A night ahead
In mangled white
A dream refuge
From daily worries

In night's nirvana
I feel so pleased
You whisper words
Of love profound

Don't wake me up
I'm bound for heaven
Don't make me face
The morning light

Just keep on flatt'ring
Just tell me lies
Make night eternal
Upon cloud nine

Don't wake me up
I'm bound for heaven
Don't make me face
The morning light

Erase all mornings
And daily struggle
When bad gets worse
And dusk remote

Don't wake me up
I'm bound for heaven
Don't make me face
The morning light

Keep on talking
In shaded darkness
To calm and comfort
My lonely heart

Echo Toy

Locate
An echo toy
Handy for
An Ego Boy

A narcissistic mirror
To use
As an ego echo
Boostering vanity

In matching teams
The two
Alternate the roles of
Reciprocal reflectors
In separate spheres

Elderly Ladies

Elderly ladies hot flashing and boiling
Their priority Toy Boys love making
Since the Flintstones they call for play
By their breath-taking efforts in bed
What a wonderful ample soft flux
Their experienced cuddling out wed
Giving pinnacle feelings deluxe
When antiques go for game to pray

On her chubby body I stay
For another lay, if I may
Her meandering curves eager to play
Her wet bush is requesting - remain
In my depth, just feel the caressing tour
Infertile delight for sure in vain
She's a modern Madame Pompadour
She is the joy for Toy Boys today

It's so great to lick those raisins tanned

To gently bite the fruit once fresh
Now fallings ripe and corset canned
For sure a cellulite stuffed rose
A coq-dive deep down in the flesh
That certain smell of fish in my nose
Excited she's screaming Oh My God
It's Bingo with five in a row

The Epiphany of the MythManiacs

Who said they were three
Who said they were kings
Who named them
Who's bones rest in Cologne

The Mid Ages mythmakers
Made a hen
Of the feather in
Mathew two one
Two and eleven

Epiphany is a Holyday
The Dome of Cologne is colossal
Caspar, Melchior and Balthazar
decorate
King Arthur's Coat of Arms and
The Swedish

A fiction has turned to a fakc fact

The Explorer

An unquiet mind
A wandering hunter
Armed with intuition
Always on the run
To or from a game
An escapist and a dreamer
Exploring and searching
For a better way
For a more exciting way
In need for triggers
Support and encouragement

Fantasy World

From a football fan
To a fantasy freak
From a ball virtuoso
To a virtual Brainiac
In Fantasy World
Ghostly characters are moving
From darkness to darkness
The space age is making
A U-turn back to
The middle ages

Fire

Hellike horniness
Senses splitting
Tortures, torments

Biheaded balmy
Masterly manipulates
Lonely lady

Wining and dining
Seduced and deceived
Warm and willing

Trembling thighs
Spreaded seeks
Erected excitement

Smell of fish
Pubic fills
Pulsing passion

Heading down
Dick deflated
Dead and drained

Evasive Eagle
Manly marks
Lines and limits

Praised Princess
Moody missing
Roses and response

For the Exes

Two empty halves
They now are through and done
Two fresh leftovers
Have parted split and run

We couldn't think
A thing to circumvent
The love we felt
It looked from heaven sent

Two caring ones
With dreams and same intends
A promise party
With dear ones and friends

It looked so firm
So sound sustainable
That perfect match
For life attainable

Our social life
A network two by two
That once were us
For singles simply no

A freedom though
To memories tied
To past and history
Unwillingly allied

Our home and things
Now scattered and split
In unknown rooms
Recycled bit by bit

Today some claim
That now we got for free
A second chance
In life's big lottery

The house we played
Our world that meant so much
Will not get back
From its echoing touch

The hearts we hurt
The day we turned the keys
And precious past
To mourning memories

The choice we made
Our fate has presumed
By love betrayed
By our destiny doomed

Same hopes, same dreams
But not in company
On our own we now
Will master our destiny

The Giant Leap

The giant leap from
Child weekly allowances
To pension payments

Golf per Verse

Short for five, buzz alarm
Wakes him up, off her arm
Still could be hour's doze
Not for him, not for those
Who are ready to go
For a round, may be two
With the clubs and the bag
Which they happily drag

Ball on peg hit like hell
Fading off hardly well
In the mist ball ends up
In the ruff far from cup
Now the game needs some sparks
Rolling wheels making marks
Bouncing ball hitting pin
One to go, who will win

Dogleg right drive with fade

Canon Club tailor made
Do the trick shooting game,
Turning left eagle aim
Far and hard off the route
Now he needs talent scout
Search and find take a chance
Glimpse of green take the stance

Put for par lift the pole
Go for hole lose control
Slapping hard on the butt
Just to keep ball on rutt
Missing cup too far gone
Score for par overdrawn
Bye bye birdie
Jot down boogey

Socket push, thicket bound
In the bush cracking sound
Out of bounds done and dead
Search for peg might be red
Score now three truly tough
Not enough uncut ruff
Deep in dirt miss again

Eight on green scoring ten

Birdies nest short par three
Not too hard could agree
Shot is good heading flag
Spinning back stops the gag
If it works will go in
Stays on track stopped by pin
It is in hole-in-one
It is done this is fun

Good Girl

Good Girl
Wants Bad Boy
With a Joy Stick
To lick

Gratitude to the Difference

Promote prosperity
Motivate multiplicity
Attentive against
Uncaring uniformity

Exchanging experience in
Dynamic debate the
Conflict creates a
Promising progress

Rational roles and
Designated duties make a
Smart symbiosis for
Engendering excellence

Invitation to Guatemala

Conversation while dancing
Translation of a song written by the poet and songwriter Evert Taube. May be an Argentinean folk song " Un lindo rancho en que yo vivo" inspired him to write "Invitation till Guatemala

I have a rancho in Guatemala
May be Miss Larsson would like to go
There I've coffee on million acres
But not a woman not one like you
I love your dimples, your cheekbones high
Your hand, your hair, your eyes so deep
A horse, a mustang I'll like to buy
You turkeys cattle and lots of sheep,
And lots of sheep, and lots of sheep

If Nordic nature with moody feelings

Would like to leave from the valley heat
You ride the mustang a few days healings
And head right up for my highland seat
Where wind is whispering in spruce and pine
You take a break for a batt'ry charge
Among the pine trees you'll feel just fine
There I have a lodge with a deck so large
With a deck so large with a deck so large

On green grass meadows the cows are guzzling
The bull looks shiny in gazing sun
And honeysuckle along the fencing
They fill the evening with fragrance hun'
And all is there and all is yours

At cosy village with shading trees
While down in valley the coffee grows
You bake our bread and make your cheese

You fancy coffee! All right! Come with me!
Enjoying muffins and Danish pastry
I want to care for you, you see
How sad Miss Larsson we act so shyly
Both you and me, but may I ask you
Will you share this kind of life?
I kindly ask you when we can go
To Guatemala as man and wife
As man and wife, as man and wife

Don Gunnardo, indeed I prize
Your kind proposal, your open mind
Although unmarried, I do have ties
I cannot leave my boy behind
How great, Miss Larsson we found the snag
You made my day, a son how fun

To be a father be proud and brag
Be young and shaved, and raise a son
And raise a son and raise a son

Yes I agree, I agree, yes I do
Just call me Lise, and what is yours
My name is Gunnar , don Gunnardo
How sweet, you are! But in the stores
In Guatemala what will be mine
Senora Larsson Gunnardin
Let’s drink to this in bubbling wine
Oh, my Gunnar, how great you are
How great you are, how great you are!

Halloween and Valentine

During Halloween
Those gone
Seek a sheltering soul
Among those not yet gone
Who try to scare them off
With creepy dresses

During Valentine
Those not yet taken
Search for a heart to fill
By dressing up
To seize
A seeking soul

Horniness

You torture, torment, wit you split, horniness
Bewildered lady still resents, birdcall tone
Biheaded layer's words and wine, gradually
Will turn her warm and willing, thanks loneliness
The trembling thighs starts spreading, twitch eagerness
Erected, firm excitement, frank plucking
A smell of fish the pubic hair fills, thrivingly
The pulsing passion penetrates, downhearted
His head turned down, deflated, drained, down-sized
Evasive eagle manly marks, borderline

The prepraised princess' moody miss,
partnership
Response and roses, recognize Lucifer

Immigrants

The path feels strange
The mountains different
The childhood memories
Stronger
The tracks of life
In the mirror
All bridges burnt behind
Home far away and
Far away home
The cultural heritage
Is a traditional disruption
The rootlessness creates
Restlessness
The walking stick is gone
The Volvo doesn't have a rear mirror
Cannot, should not
Look backwards

In Our World

In our world
There is my world
And your world
The family world
The friends' world
The work world
Groups and cultures
They all have rules
To act by and we play
Different roles

In Search for Excellence

Something better
Around the corner
A shortcut
A smarter
Solution
Dumping existing
For the new
Constantly

The Inner Circle

The inner circle
In need for a hero
In need for an enemy
Making up its own rules
Cocooning
Cut off from external influence
Whose laws are applicable
And who is the judge

The Light in the Tunnel. Haikku

The light at the end
Of the tunnel is the light
From the train on time

John Walker Lind

Bewildered youngster
Searching for identity
A group of peers
Isolated, separated, unintegrated

Missionaries seeking prospects
Like hunting lions
For weakest in the flock
To catch and poison
To catch and to conquer
Missionary and misfit match

Join our congregation
We offer friendship
And an identity
We answer your questions
We take care of you
And we care for you

Truth offered and delivered
JWL is receptive
A fast learner
And soon fascinated,
indoctrinated and caught

Under social control JWL
Is tied and imprisoned
An integrated member of a
Weird organization with

A special role to fulfil
Well prepared for
Mercenary missions

Ready, willing and able
To kill for causa nostra
Old friends or new enemies
Make the same
A robot is programmed
Beyond ability
To take responsibility for
His own actions

Under social control JWL
Is tied and imprisoned
An integrated member of a
Weird organization with

A special role to fulfil
Well prepared for
Mercenary missions

Ready, willing and able
To kill for causa nostra
Old friends or new enemies
Make the same
A robot is programmed
Beyond ability
To take responsibility for
His own actions

A potential murderer is
Formed
Beyond a toolings ability
To understand the operation
He is used for
Dehumanising an enemy

Beyond social norms

JWL is just like any KuKluxKlan
member
Mob, McCarty or MRA for that matter

Lady Bird

Wise like an owl
Sweet like a hummingbird
Sharp-eyed like an eagle
Rare like a kingfisher
Determined like a woodpecker
Caring like a redwing
Noble like a penguin

Lie To Me Dear

If you don't love me, Dear,
Just lie to me
Whisper wonderful words in my ear
I'll believe whatever you say
Just for the feeling
Lie to me, Dear
Tell me we'll never part
Tell me more lies
Like I'm someone special
Like you and I
Are The Dream Team
Just tell me you love me
Who's to tell what's true
What's the truth
Against the feeling of being loved
A badly needed feeling

Life

Morning stress and eve routine
Hair drier and laundry loads
Vacuum buzz and dirty dishes
All these days
Just passing
Who could imagine
They were Life
Too many goodbyes
Too few nice-to-see-you
A glimpse alive
Heading for eternity
Too few quickies
Too many naggies
Too little quality time
Too much wasted

Limerick Charkiv

A Lady from city Charkiv
FaceBook has her in the archive
In head well equipped
For sure when stripped
With legs spread super attractive

Love

Love is kind of gambling
With the risk of loosing
Pay the entrance fee
By surrender
Love is kind of surprise
Erase the diary note
Love is a drunken driver
Out of control
Who finds beauty
The object may miss
Love drains
Even for Superwoman
Love adapts
To circumstances

Lullabye

A nite ahead
With guts to sleep
Away from self
And daily worry
A dream refuge
In mangled white

The daily record
Processed at sleep
The monotonous
And rhythmic tender
Replace the plans
At nite's nirvana

The shaded darkness
Seclusion curtain
For cupid sessions
And shared cure
Conveys the warmth

When sun falls short

The daily struggle
Just fades away
For change of stage
iI nightly orbit
With roles reversed
In virtual play

A wraith of sleep
In waiting line
For darker days
When bad gets worse
With dawn remote
And no escape

Men from Mars Women from Venus

Bewildered Venus
Seeks security
Lonely looking
For monogamous millionaire

Polygamous playboy
Pleased by the plentiful
Flagging for freedom
Resenting relations

Woman from Venus
Man from Mars
Routed roads
Separate spheres

Matching mates
Occasional occurrence
Coincidental crossings

The Lottery of Life

Man from Mars
Woman wants
Warm and willing
Humble and horny

Frustrated female's
Fatal phantom
Reliable relationship
Tango for two

Mismatch

How could a perfect match
Turn to a mismatch
A tearing ambiguity of
Missing and too much
Where free
Wants tied and
Tied
Wants free
How could staying be a burden
And leaving same burden

Mix

I love to mix
The mixer is my favorite tool
Gazpazzo with shrimps and sausage
Love for brunch
I love the change
Variety is the spice of life
Love to have many things going on at the same time
Love to be a dilettante

My Beauty

The line of your lips
The dimples in your chin
Your high cheek bones
Makes me heavenly bound

Your glittering eyes
Your chubby thighs
Your sex appeal
Makes him take off

Your compassion
Your gentle mind
Your caring character
Makes me marry you

My Man

Inspired by Leonard Cohen's "I'm Your Man"
and "Fields of Joy" by an unknown writer
This is from her side when she claims "My Man"

On my way through life
I feel it's getting close
My Man will come along
He'll slowly tune me in,
And make me sense and hear
A long-forgotten song

He'll come to know me
From inside and from out
The special one that's Me
He'll like me for the good
And all that's not so good
Whatever that might be

He’ll gently find and learn
The shaded side of me
Where no one was to go
For sure he'll be part of me
My mate and better me
And much I like him to

He'll take me through the day
No matter what I've done
He’ll nurse me through the night
‘til dawn breaks the day
Together side by side
Our day is turning bright

In joy he'll be there
A partner and a friend
To share smile and laughter
To be my kindred spirit
To be my better me
For rainy days and after

He’ll take me by the hand,
And just the two of us
Find places one can't see
The whole wide world around
And everywhere we go
He’ll mean the world to me

He’ll make me feel I am
a very special one
He’ll make me leave the ground
He’ll make my dreams come true
My inmost hopes fulfilled
A life that’s heavenly bound

As time goes by the ties
Will make me understand
The words unspoken
He’s me and I am him
Between us sensing
The very smallest token

He’s honest, faithful, true
Which matters much to me
I'm glad he came to share
a world so small which now
is great with dreams and hope
of which he too takes care

A happy, grateful me
For precious trust and joy
And just for being there
A very thankful thought
To caring guardian angels
For willingness to share

The Network

Dear ones pass away
Friends disappear
Few Hi there
The network vanish

The friendly dialogue turns to
A mumbling mourning monologue
Watching the TV test picture
Another weekend hell ahead

The loneliness finds
An escape route by
Maniac misuse of
Addictive alternatives

No Dancing

There are four good things in life
Golf and brandy, money and weed
If you look for something confusing
A woman will be all you need

A woman doesn't say what she wants
You are somehow supposed to know
If she wants to do this or that
Stay here or there or just go

No wonder you regard her heart
Just another playing thing
That she wants to have broken
Like a secret or her angle wing

You have an urge to dismantle
To see what make things go around
Same when it comes to making love
You volunteer just to hear the sound

To fall in love, my friend
it takes a lot of nerve
It takes a special kind of blond
to perform what you deserve

You never give your heart away
You play the woman for a fool
You wait until she gives her heart
And then you play it very cool

Oh How Lovely This Sensation

Oh how lovely this sensation
Hairy pussy wet and small
Biting nipples turning upwards
Moaning cum and yelling loud
Multi cascading orgasms
Wetting coq and Kingsize bed
Blissouts we are feeling
Close to heaven as we are

Our Daily Jigsaw

Our daily jigsaw doings
On mandatory rails
From dawn to dusk
Wandering through life in
A labyrinth of paths
To the right or to the left
Doesn’t matter
The dead ends are
Just part of the road
Finally ending
Sheer down

Our Pleasure

Eyes sparkle
Breasts nipple
Bottom beauty
Warm and willing

Hot lips
Deep down tongues
Impatiently licking
Buttock touch

Body close to body
Excited eager
Finds slit in
Soaked fur

Gentle euphony for
Mutual pleasure in
Synchronized climax
Locking legs beg for more

The Paradise of the Planet For Alice the Alcoholic

The believers think
That Paradise is in Heaven
But you know
It's here and now
You open your Eden
At any cost
To find bliss
Far from rough reality
Do you always win
In this lottery
My tickets
Just bring hangovers
You who know
Share your secret
The world is waiting

Passion

Passion has a price
It occupies you
It takes your time
Your energy
It makes you feel apart
Blindfolds you

Peace and Freedom

In Summer heat
The day has ended
And twilight calm
Is now extended
To lakes and air
To fields and forest
In peace and freedom
Enjoying rest
On cottage stairs
A rare moment
When thoughts keep flying
And life looks decent
Just swallow's switching
My mind distracting
At time and places
And those impacting
Perceived perspectives
In solitude
They fill my spirit

With gratitude
It's missing nothing
No special one
Regrets could be
And done undone
With moisture rising
In deepening darkness
The body missing
Somebody’s warmness

Pet, the

A pet is
Active and alert
Playful and loving
Warm and affectionate
Faithful and passionate
May be some day

Pussytin

A clown in Kremlin
A hen with coq
In macho torso
For the clown Pussytin et consortes
Politics is a disguise for
Greediness
Nouveau rich have no traditions for
Exercising power
Without oil revenues
No financial means
Europe rearms
The noose is tightened
The sanctions hurts
The ordinary citizen

Raisa

Beautiful and beneficial
Empathetic and exhibitionistic
Up nosed shy and
Cocksure unsure
Low self-confidence with
High life expectations

Restless

A restless soul finds no rest
Driven by an inner engine
In search for something better
In search for someone better
Never looking backwards
Without guilt, without regrets
Always going for the dream

The Revolution

A real lunatic
Irrational and unpredictable
It claims its tribute
Without guarantees
It sees no shortcomings
It blinds and betrays
It cannot be controlled
Or managed
It sees beauty and loveliness
Where neither may be found
It is handy and useful
Realizing the beneficial
It fills all of you
Occupying your soul and body
It appears in many natures
As time goes by

Rule Britannia Rule

Rule Britannia Rule
We are still strong and cool
Even if only 36 % voted for Brexit
For sure we want our exit
May be our internal turmoil
Can be our new export coil
We don't need Brussels
We have our own muscles
Finding other associates and partners
Other markets and kindergartners
We oldies remember the good old days
Which the youngsters don't praise

Brussels will welcome Scotland
Then bye bye UK
For sure EC is as big as US
But there are other markets equally big
EC was Churchill's vision in 1945

Memories are short

Rules. Haikku

One playground, two teams
Making rules of their own
Not a winning squad

Rhythm and rhyme

Rhythm and rhyme
Is a matter of time
The idea is artwork
The rest is labor
Wrap it up and
Wrap it in
Rap it up

Roadblocks

Not a perfect match
But it works
Neutralizing uneasiness
In many ways impossible
A kind of life in a lifeboat
Drifting and in between
The twosomeness
Comforts the loneliness

An attachment
Not exactly wanted
Like a personal belonging
With someone's nametag on
Tied to a network of
Acquaintances
One involvement
Blocks another

It takes courage to leave the

Institutional security
To make the constructive
Destructive move
To detach
To walk on
Freed and free

A new set of buttons pushed
A new match interacting
With that certain feeling
With that certain hope
The vicious circle broken
And a new one started
From one attachment
To another

The Road Sign

It shows the way from
Its road side vision
The way it never went
They show us the way
The preachers
The politicians
The professors
By their show-them-the-road passion

7 Female Wonders

Her nippy wits
Her stiff nipples
Her divine desire
Her beautiful bottom
Her enormous empathy
Her prudent personality
Her double-jointed jungle

Side by side

I want to sing
The same song you sing
I want to walk
The pace you walk
I want to share
Your day and your world
To be your man and your pride
Eternally by your side
Together towards
The Promise land

Small Ponds and Open Sea

Simple and sound
Tolerant and tranquil
Beautiful and beneficial
Positive and progressive
Capable and considerate
Sensitive and sophisticated
Magnificent and metropolitan

Stout and sloppy
Dull and disordered
Rural and restricted
Queer and questioning
Complex and confusing
Boring and bothersome
Provoking and protesting

Solidarity

Solidarity
With environment and pets
With neglected and rejected
With concern and with care
To nothing committing
The farther the better
But never a penny for
A neighbour in need

The Sugarholic

The true sugarholic
Is like an alcoholic
Driven by abstinence
When - by accident
Or when stressed
The sweet tooth wants
More of the desserts
Fattening and destructive
Fatal and seductive
For teeth and for heart
Each lump a jumpstart
Heading six feet under
For sure no wonder
This serial killer
Going on like a caterpillar
Should be a licensed item
Could bc a way to fight 'em

The Surprise of the Year

The surprise of the year
No Nobel Prize oh Dear
If Mrs. Arnault had done what expected
Jean-Claude's hadn't been erected
And other problems neglected
A horny frog
Sticky like a hedgehog
Send him to hell
There he can dwell
But for sue not here
Let him disappear

There is something rotten
in the Republic of Russia

In Isvestia no pravda
In Pravda no isvestia
No free press
No free word
No free internet
Dictators are moneymakers
Hitler died as a very rich man
And so will Putin

The Taliban. Haikku

Eighty-six virgins
Waiting the suicidal
Horny Taliban

Variety

My best friend is a gorgeous girl
For sure she's a genuine pearl
I fully understand you
If you want her and let me go
And then I will have two best friends
No way our relation ends
My friend has someone special too
A very good man indeed
A real man that I may need
Let's make this unexpected swap
Without hesitation and stop
Maybe he wants me as his wife
Variety is the spice of life
Variety is the spice of life

Test men 'til you get the right one
That is how it should be done
Why settle with a bloke next best
Let him shortly rest by your chest

If he is not good enough
Be really tough and get rough
And go hard for the next sport
Relationships should be short

Go for the perfect counterpart
Until death do you two apart
The right man is good at small talk
At the table and at walk
The man who will be your pride
Good to have him by your side
When life gets tricky
And pals get sticky
He's for sure one in a million
A good father for your children
And super in bed
He is the one to wed

When You Think That Everything Is Past and Gone

When you think that everything is past
and gone
And in darkness feel you are past done
That's the moment you have to fight
Even if it's cold and you see no light
Afterwards you'll realize
That just at sunrise
The night is cold and stinging
Then the birds start singing

Translation of a poem written by
the Swedish poet Mr. Harry Blomberg

Why worry

Jobless and homeless
Mistrust and distrust
Apathy in futility

The Social control
Eliminated

Suddenly some action

Why bother

No dream
No aim
No future

Another boost
Towards polarization
We and them

World Championship

Bottoms up for
Ladies' Pool Jump
A fascinating sport
Requiring
Skill and strength
Brilliant for
Bottomspotters

Worship

My dearest divine
I love the goldmine
In your slender panties
It makes me vigilantes
Your asstronomic avec
A fabulous heck
Your tight triangle
Penetrated without wrangle
Your volcano orgasms
Glad that I got'ems
When your skirt falls
There are no walls
The heaven is exposed
The paradise disclosed

Your Beauty

Your Beauty, My Dear
Will disappear
What will remain
Is your Brain
Between your ears
And the Treasure
Our True pleasure
Between your legs
For which he begs

www.ingramcontent.com/pod-product-compliance
Lightning Source LLC
LaVergne TN
LVHW010110170826
845678LV00012B/2323

* 9 7 9 8 6 6 8 0 6 7 2 6 8 *